Six-Dinner Sid

Aladdin Paperbacks
An imprint of Simon & Schuster
Children's Publishing Division
1230 Avenue of the Americas
New York, NY 10020
Copyright © 1991 by Inga Moore
Originally published in Great Britain by Simon & Schuster Young Books
All rights reserved including the right of reproduction
in whole or in part in any form.
Also available in a hardcover edition from Simon & Schuster Books for Young Readers

Printed and bound in Belgium by Proost International Book Production

10 9 8 7 6 5 4 3

Library of Congress Cataloging-in-Publication Data

Moore, Inga. Six-dinner Sid. Summary: Sid the cat plays the pet
of six different owners on Aristotle Street so that he
can get six dinners every night. [1. Cats—Fiction.]
I. Title. II. Title: 6-dinner Sid. PZ7.M7846S1 1991 [E]—dc20 90-42749

ISBN: 0-671-79613-5

Six-Dinner Sid

by Inga Moore

Aladdin Paperbacks

Sid lived at number one Aristotle Street.

He also lived at number two, number three,
number four, number five, and number six.

Sid lived in six houses so that he could have
six dinners. Each night he would slip out
of number one, where he might have
had chicken, into number
two for fish…

on to number three for lamb

liver at number four

fish again at number five…

ending at number six
with beef-and-kidney stew.

Since the neighbors did not talk to each other on Aristotle Street, they did not know what Sid was up to. They all believed the cat they fed was theirs, and theirs alone.

But Sid had to work hard
for his dinners. It wasn't
easy being six people's pet.
He had six different names
to remember and six
different ways to behave.

When he was being
Scaramouche, Sid put
on swanky airs.

As Bob he had a job.

He was naughty as Mischief…

and silly as Sally.

As Sooty he smooched…

but as Schwartz he had to act rough and tough.

All this work sometimes wore Sid out. But he didn't care, as long as he had his six dinners. And, besides, he liked being…

scratched in six different places…

and sleeping in six different beds.

In fact, life on Aristotle Street
was just about perfect for Sid,
until...

one cold, damp day, he caught a nasty cough.

The next thing he knew,
he was being taken to the vet.
Poor Sid, he was taken not once…

not twice...

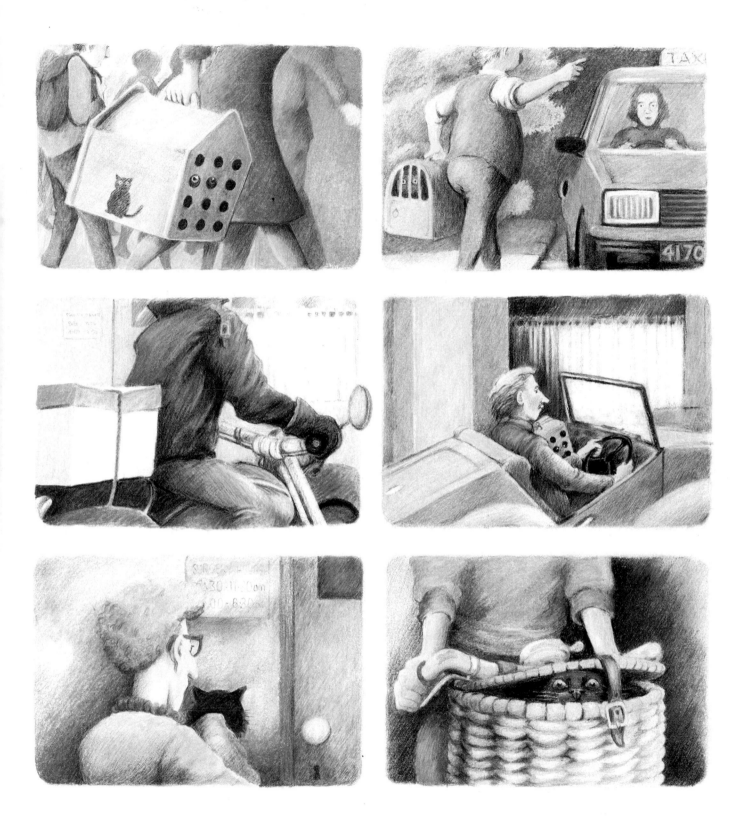

but six times!
He went with six different people,
in six different ways.

The vet said Sid's cough wasn't nearly as nasty
as it sounded; but, to be on the safe side,
he should have a spoonful of medicine.

Of course,
Sid didn't have just one
spoonful of medicine.

He had six!

Now, one black cat does look much like another; but nobody, not even a busy vet, could see the same cat six times without becoming suspicious. Sure enough, when he checked in his appointment book, the vet found six cats with a cough—all living on Aristotle Street!

So he called the owners at once…

and, oh dear, Sid was found out!
When they discovered what he had been up to,
Sid's owners said he had no business eating so
many dinners.

They said, in the future, they would make sure
he had only one dinner a day.

But Sid was a six–dinner–a–day cat. So he went to live
at number one Pythagoras Place. He also went to live
at numbers two, three, four, five, and six.

Unlike Aristotle Street, the people who
lived on Pythagoras Place talked to
their neighbors.
So, right from the start, everyone
knew about Sid's six dinners.

And, because everyone knew,
nobody minded.